It was the day before winter break and Atticus's friends were happily discussing their Christmas plans.

Atticus grinned. He absolutely loved Christmas. It was the one time of year he could always count on seeing his grandparents, Yiayia and Papou, who lived too far away to visit often.

"We always fly to Colorado," Millie said. "Then I wake up really early Christmas morning and play in the snow. I can't wait!"

"We don't celebrate Christmas," said Fatima, whose family had just PCS'ed from Morocco. "What are some of your favorite Christmas traditions?"

# THE MILITARY CHILD CHRONICLES

Written by
**Athens E. Pellegrino**

Illustrated by
**Cody Taylor**

For my beloved mother, who always made
Christmas special, no matter what.

ISBN 978-1-7365126-3-0

Layout design by Ryan Durnford, edited by Brooke Vitale

Atticus thought back to last Christmas...
stringing up holiday lights, baking cookies,
making gingerbread houses, seeing *Santa!*

"I love everything!" he shouted.

Heading inside, Atticus gave Callista
a big hug. "Where's Mommy?"
he asked.

Then he heard her. Peering
into the living room, he saw her
pacing and talking on her phone.
She nervously smiled at him.

Atticus looked at Callista, but she was too busy playing with the dogs to notice him. Behind him, Mommy hung up the phone and sighed.
"What's wrong, Mommy?" Atticus asked.

Mommy bent down and took Atticus's hands.

"I'm sorry, honey, but it's looking like Yiayia and Papou won't be able to make it for Christmas this year, after all. There's a huge blizzard coming and all the airports are being closed."

"But..." Atticus gasped. Tears filled his eyes and ran down his cheeks. "How will we celebrate without them?" he said softly, wiping his eyes. "Christmas is ruined!"

"Oh, Atticus," Mommy said, pulling him close. "I know it feels that way now, but I promise, it will be okay. I bet there are a lot of people whose plans have just changed. I'll tell you what: Let's think of what we should do for the holidays. We'll create a mission."

Grabbing a roll of paper, Mommy spread it on the table. The children were quiet for a moment, then all of a sudden Atticus bellowed, "Can we have a big Christmas party here?!"

"Ummm... let me ask your—"

Before Mommy could finish her sentence, Atticus and Callista grabbed her hands and pulled. "Please, Mommy! Please!"

"Of course we can!" a deep voice said.

It was Daddy, home from work. The children ran to him for huge hugs and kisses. "Ah, we've got a new mission, huh? Well, what are you going to name it?" Daddy asked.

Atticus stared up at the decoration hanging in the entryway. Then, a gigantic smile forming on his face, he shouted, "MISSION: MISTLETOE! On the count of 3, everyone yell MISTLETOE! 1-2-3!"

"MISTLETOE!" the whole family roared.

"Mission: Mistletoe it is!" Mommy said.

"Now what do we need?"

 Buy a roll of plain paper. Make homemade wrapping paper by stamping, painting, and coloring. For holiday cards and gift tags, reuse cards from previous years, family photos, glitter, ribbon, and buttons.

While Mommy wrote down ideas, Daddy and Atticus drew out an invitation. When they were done, they rolled up several copies like small telegrams to deliver.

"Anything else?" Mommy asked.

"Miss-toe!" Callista replied, and pirouetted across the kitchen.

FAMILY ACTIVITY

*Organize a holiday party on a large or small scale. Come up with some entertainment ideas, like an ornament exchange, cookie decorating, lip-sync contest, and holiday movie marathon. For more ideas, see The Military Child Chronicles official website.*

The next morning, Atticus woke up early and put
on his pilot hat and goggles. Piling the invitations
into his backpack, he headed outside.
"Ready?" Daddy asked. "Hooah!" Atticus replied.
He pulled down his goggles and off they went!

When all the invitations had been delivered, Atticus and Daddy made their way home.
"That was fun!" Atticus said.
"I wonder what Mommy and Callista–"

Atticus stopped short at the sound of clanging metal and Mom shouting, "Oh no. No, oh dear!"

Stepping into the kitchen, he saw
Mom and Callista both covered from
head to toe in flour.
"What happened?!" he asked.
"Miss-toe!" Callista said, and took a
bite out of a cookie.

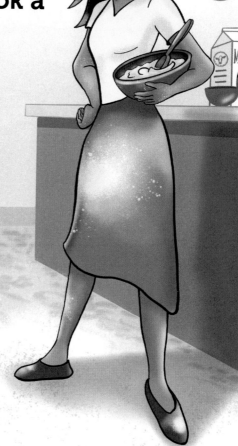

FAMILY ACTIVITY

*Create a cookie exchange! Bake your favorite holiday cookies, separate onto plates, and label the plate with your recipe. Swap with neighbors.*

After dinner, Daddy led the family into the backyard.
"Surprise!" he said. Atticus gasped, his body filling
with excitement. The whole yard was covered in bright
Christmas lights.

# Beside him, Callista danced around shouting, "Miss-toe! Miss-toe!"

**FAMILY ACTIVITY**

*Set up a hot chocolate buffet! Include hot cocoa mix, marshmallows, candy canes, chocolate chips, whipped cream, sprinkles, and cookies. Enjoy!*

HAPPY HOLIDAYS!

A C A C

The next morning, Atticus woke up and ran into Callista's room.

"Good morning, mistletoe!" he whispered.

"Miss-toe!" Callista repeated, and chased him downstairs.

At the bottom of the steps, Atticus stopped. Mommy and Daddy had been busy! The house was a magnificent, magical, winter wonderland! It smelled of pine and cinnamon, and mistletoe hung in every doorway.

Looking around, Atticus had an idea. "Mommy, can you help me with a surprise for Millie?"

Later that evening, Atticus and Callista stood in the front room waiting for their friends. Millie's family was the first to arrive. "I have something to show you!" Atticus said. Taking Millie's hand, he led her inside.

Millie's jaw dropped as she looked at the snowflakes hanging from the ceiling. Millie hugged Atticus tight. "Wowwww! I get to see snow after all! Oh, Atticus, thank you!" Atticus grinned. "Merry Christmas, Millie!"

*Schedule a time with distant family and friends for a video call. Exchange gifts virtually, bake the same recipe, and/or read a holiday book together!*

Across the yard, Atticus saw their other neighbors shuffling toward the house.

"MISSION: MISTLETOE... EXECUTE!" he yelled.

Soon, everyone on base was laughing, eating, and dancing like one big, happy, family.

Suddenly, Atticus heard the sound of sleigh bells. "He's here! Santa's here!" he shouted. The guests rushed outside. Above them, a helicopter circled the base.

It was Santa! He was waving from the doorway of the helicopter. Below him, an elf dangled on a ladder!

"Special orders from the North Pole," the elf called. "All the children must hurry and get to bed soon! Santa is on his way!"

Atticus frowned. He wanted Santa to come, but he didn't want the party to end. He was having so much fun.

Then Atticus realized something. Christmas *had* been different this year. He missed Yiayia and Papou, but everyone there was his family, too.

His magnificent military family!

And being with them was a wonderful way to celebrate his favorite holiday.

MISSION: MISTLETOE, COMPLETE!